Library of Congress Cataloging in Publication Data

Reesink, Marijke, 1919– The princess who always ran away.
Translation of Het prinsesje dat altijd wegliep.
Summary: An overprotective king seeks a way to prevent
his youngest daughter from leaving the castle.
[1. Princesses—Fiction] I. Trésy, Françoise, 1943– II. Title.
PZ7.R2554Pr [E] 80-16849
ISBN 0-07-051714-2

First published in the United States of America 1981
by McGraw-Hill Book Company.
First published in the Netherlands 1980
by Lemniscaat b.v., Rotterdam.

The Princess Who Always Ran Away

story by Marijke Reesink • pictures by Françoise Trésy

McGraw-Hill Book Company

New York St. Louis San Francisco

THE KING'S CASTLE stood tall and high, overlooking the wooded hills and the sea that roared nearby. The castle had many towers and spacious halls. Stairs led up to the highest tower and down to the deepest cellar.

Surrounding the castle was a moat, deep and wide. In the castle and on the walls outside were soldiers and sentries and watchmen who guarded every entryway and every exit.

The King was a severe master: everyone had to obey him—but there was one who didn't.

The King had seven daughters. They could draw and paint beautifully. They loved to play music and they made the finest embroidery.

These daughters were well behaved, and their lovely clothes were always neat and tidy. They always obeyed their father—all seven of them.

But there was another daughter, the eighth and youngest. She did not like to wear beautiful clothes, nor to sit and make music, nor to embroider. In fact she didn't like to be closed up indoors.

She loved to roam freely outdoors, where she would climb trees and run about barefoot; or just to lie lazily in the grass and watch the birds and the butterflies, the snails and the spiders.

Her sisters tried to persuade her to be more like them and not disturb their father. But she couldn't help herself.

She wasn't really naughty at heart, she was just different, very different. And that was exactly what the King her father did not permit.

Whenever the King's servants stood for a moment chatting among themselves, or when a sentry had to sneeze and close his eyes for a moment, the little princess whisked away and was gone.

She knew dozens of hiding places in the woods around the castle. There she would remain for hours or even for days.

The King would order his servants and soldiers to look for her. And usually they would find her sleeping in the wilds and bring her back. And then the King would be angry and punish her.

One day the little princess had again been sent to her room—without dinner—for running away. There she sat, thinking how she could escape. Evening came and she was still sitting and thinking. And when it was night and the narrow yellow sickle of the moon rose, the princess was still awake.

Nothing stirred in the castle. The little princess opened her door very softly. There was no one in sight. Careful to make no noise, she went down the long, long staircase, down to the deepest, darkest cellar.

There, she knew, was an old rotten door. She pulled hard and the door opened. It led to a narrow corridor. At its end she saw the moon, and she jumped and danced for joy. She was free once again! She got herself wet and dirty in the woods, and she was happy.

But the King's guards found her a few days later. And when they brought her back to her father, the King was very, very angry indeed.

He had the little princess shut up in the highest tower. The windows were barred, and the key was turned seven times in the lock.

There she sat all alone, with only one thought. How could she get out?

Then the little princess had an idea.

She took the rugs and her bedspread, the blankets, sheets, and pillowcase and tied them together. Then she attached her dresses, belts, and underwear—they made a very long rope.

She tied the rope to the bars, squeezed through them, and slid down the rope from the high tower window to the moat far below.

She swam across the moat and went straight to her most secret hiding place. There she stayed for three days and three nights feeding on blackberries.

But on the fourth day, when she was trying to pick wild apples, she was caught by one of the King's soldiers.

This time the King was furious. When the soldier brought the little princess to him, her father glared at her and said, "You love freedom too much. It's time you learned a lesson, daughter."

He ordered a huge ball to be made, and when it was ready he ordered that the princess be brought to him again.

"I am going to seal you inside this ball, daughter," the King said.

"Do you want to take any food?" "No," said the princess.

"Do you want to take your bed?" "No."

"Do you want your toys and dolls?" "No."

"Then what do you want to take with you?" "NOTHING."

But hidden under her skirts she had a pair of scissors, a dagger, and an axe.

The King ordered his men to put the princess inside the ball.

On a wagon drawn by four strong horses the ball was taken to the sea. An anchor was attached to it. Weighed down by the heavy chain, it sank to the bottom of the sea.

Early the next morning a heavy mist blanketed the sea. A lone fisherman was hauling in his net. But the net caught hold of the anchor chain, and the fisherman pulled it up with great difficulty. Then the ball floated to the surface. The fisherman used all his strength to tow the ball to the shore, some distance away.

The King's servants could not find the ball or the chain or the anchor when the King sent them to retrieve the ball the next day. The King was sure his daughter had learned her lesson by then.

The servants were very dejected when they went back to the King, for in their hearts they all loved the little princess. So, indeed, did the King.

Inside the ball, the princess had felt the wagon shaking when it was taken to the sea. She had heard the waves lapping when the ball was thrown in, and she had noticed the dead silence when the ball rested on the bottom of the sea.

Then she heard the voice of the fisherman talking to himself as lonely people will do. There was movement again, and the lapping of waves.

"I may be free yet!" she cried.

She took the scissors and tried to open the seams—but the scissors were too small.

Then she grasped the dagger and thrust it into the sides with all her might. But the ball was too strong.

Finally she took the axe, and swinging it heartily she managed to make a hole large enough to squeeze out.

The fisherman, in the meantime, had grown more and more frightened of the miraculous ball he had brought ashore. He saw the terrible dragon painted on the side. It had a wicked eye and sharp teeth.

When he heard the princess's cry and the noise of the axe, he thought it was the dragon threatening him.

"Silence!" he shouted, "or I will throw you back into the sea!"

Just at that moment the little princess tumbled out.

The little princess laughed when she heard the fisherman.

"No," she said, "you needn't throw me back. I am free now to go where I like, to dance in the woods, and to sleep in the wild!"

She smiled at the fisherman, who was young and handsome.

She gave him just one kiss and then ran away.

Nobody—not the King, nor her seven sisters, nor the servants, soldiers, sentries, or guards, nor even the fisherman—has ever seen the little princess since. But someday, when you are out in the woods, if you should meet a slender, barefooted girl in a torn dress, singing and laughing at the birds, that just might be her....